The cobbler mends and sells boots. It is a hard job.

I0816411

"It is such a problem," the cobbler thinks. "I need to mend and sell boots to earn coins for food and rent, but I must sleep."

It is dark and still in the cobbler's store.

The cobbler and his family are asleep.

A cheeky elf skips into the cobbler's store and jumps onto the moonlit desk.

He picks up a hammer and some nails.

A second little elf skips in and jumps onto the moonlit desk.

She picks up some pins and needles.

The elves begin to cut, fix, hammer, and stitch.

They forget about the noise.

The cobbler is up! He is hidden in a dark corner of the store.

The cobbler can see the little elves, but they cannot see him.

The sun is up. The elves run quickly out of the cobbler's store and vanish.

They have left hundreds and hundreds of boots for the cobbler to sell.

"We will be rich!" the cobbler tells his family.

The cobbler and his family proudly sell all of the boots.

They get lots and lots of cash!

The cobbler and his family wish to thank the elves.

They stitch little outfits with teeny-weeny boots as a gift.

The cobbler and his family are hidden in a dark corner of the store.

“We will never forget,” the cobbler whispers as they see the elves jump around happily.